The Girl with the Raven Tongue

Greenland Missing Persons #2

featuring Constable Petra "Piitalaat" Jensen

Don't miss novella #3 in the
Greenland Missing Persons series
The Shiver in the Arctic

Introduction

The Girl with the Raven Tongue is another purely fictional story to which I have added generous amounts of dramatic license. The settlement of Kangaamiut does exist, but the characters and events in this story are of my own fabrication. Kangaamiut is one of the most picturesque places you can visit in Greenland.

This story is the second in a series of novellas in which we follow Constable Petra Jensen, as she investigates missing persons cases in Greenland. Each story features returning characters, and charts Petra's early career on the Greenlandic police force.

These stories are cosier than the novels featuring Petra and the dour but dependable Constable David Maratse. They are set prior to the events in the novels starting with *Seven Graves, One Winter*, and before the trilogy of Greenland thrillers of which *The Ice Star* is the first.

If you're new to my Greenland crime stories, you can read these novellas without a deeper knowledge of the semi-fictional Greenland in which they are set. You might, however, want to start with the first novella in this series: *The Boy with the Narwhal*

Tooth.

Chris
July 2020
Denmark

The Girl with the Raven Tongue

Greenland Missing Persons #2

Part 1

There is something exhilarating about preparing for the Friday night shift in Greenland's capital city of Nuuk. You can see it in the faces of the officers as they prepare for the evening. I'm pretty sure the novelty will wear off quickly. But there is a camaraderie among my colleagues, a strong bond that helps all of us get through the night. Even Sergeant Kiiu "George" Duneq, with his ample stomach squeezed within the constraints of his police utility belt is quick to share a jest or jibe, something to spice up the moment, and make everyone laugh. I want to laugh along with them, but each time I try, even a creasing of my lips, Sergeant Jowls, as I call him, does his best to wipe the smile from my face.

"Training is over, Jensen."

It's his stock response, his one-liner designed to put me in my place and remind me of his, every single time. I get it. I really do. I understand I still have so much to learn, but by my reckoning one more Friday night brings me closer to that goal.

"Yes, Sergeant," I said. There was nothing else to say. There never is.

"I'm splitting you up tonight." He waddled over to where Atii Napa and I were getting ready. "You and Napa spend too much time with each other as it is."

I didn't believe that, and the look on Atii's face confirmed it. Since graduating the police academy, we had hardly seen one another, at least not as much as we would like to.

"Napa is with Sergeant Alatak tonight," Jowls said. "Jensen, you're with me."

Atii fought back a snicker until Jowls was gone, then let it out with a snort she caught in the sleeve of her jacket.

"Not fair, Atii," I said.

"You should see your face."

"You should see *yours*."

We both knew that putting Atii together with Sergeant Gaba Alatak was asking for trouble, she had been mooning over him for weeks. But for me, *another* night in the company of Sergeant Jowls, was torture, made worse by the fact that he knew it, just like he knew Atii fancied Gaba.

"We'll see each other at midnight," Atii said, slapping my arm on the way out the door.

Of course, we would, I thought, knowing that one of the bars closed at midnight, and that was likely to be the first flashpoint of the night, drawing as many officers to that location as were available. That's when I'd be bound to see Atii, but not for much more than a smile, or a nod, before we started ducking elbows and *helping* patrons on their way to the next watering hole. Some would go home; others would go to jail. It was just never clear who would end up where.

Before heading out of the office I cast one last wistful glance at my desk at the far end, tucked beneath a staircase. If the telephone rang before I started my evening shift, I would have a good excuse to postpone my patrol with Jowls. Of course, it didn't. You can't just *will* someone to disappear, at least, not that I was aware of. The phone didn't ring. I was all out of excuses, and it was time to get my butt into the car, maybe even the driving seat, although that was, generally, asking too much of Jowls. Unless he had a point to make.

The duty officer turned the volume up on the television mounted to the wall, slowing my way out of the door. We both stared at the sight of the Danish Royal Air Force Challenger jet streaking over the town of Maniitsoq, north of Nuuk, just south of the Arctic Circle. Apart from flying sovereignty missions – about which I knew next to nothing – the Challenger aircraft was used in Search and Rescue missions, when the weather, ice conditions, or geography, often all three, prevented police and volunteers from searching. The aircraft had powerful cameras that could cover large areas quickly. I had seen the footage on television and been amazed at the detail.

Of course, if the plane was flying over Maniitsoq on a Friday night in early spring, then the chances were high that someone was…

"…missing," said the duty officer. "A little girl. Last seen walking alone into the mountains."

"Alone?"

"Yep."

"How old?"

"Eleven." The duty officer, another sergeant, shook his head. "Forget it, Jensen. She's missing,

8

but it's not an actual missing persons case. Not yet, anyway. It's too soon." He jabbed his finger towards the door. "Better get a move on. Duneq is waiting."

"I know," I said, with another glance at the television. The news camera crew from *Kalaallit Nunaata Radioa,* zoomed back to focus on the reporter as she explained the circumstances, while pointing at a distraught woman in the background of the shot. The reporter spoke in Greenlandic. I knew she would repeat it all again in Danish, but I couldn't wait, Jowls was already in the car. "Let me know what happens," I said, as I headed for the door.

"You might have a desk, Jensen," the duty officer said. "But I'm not your secretary."

I thought about saying something in return, but teasing among colleagues only went so far. I was still pretty green when it came to experience. Besides, a Friday night shift on payday was no time to let my mind wander. The little girl would have to wait. I just hoped it wouldn't be long before they found her; in the news report clip the girl's mother looked close to breaking point.

"Jensen, get a move on."

"Yes, Sergeant."

I jogged for the door, adjusting my belt, and repositioning my pistol holster over my hip, as Sergeant Duneq pointed at the driver's seat.

I almost smiled.

It had been raining since midday, and now, with a sudden drop in temperature, the conditions were perfect to test Duneq's favourite constable.

"More training," I breathed, as I opened the driver's door. "Until it's over."

I adjusted the mirrors and the seat, nodded once to Jowls, and then started the car.

The Friday night shift had begun.

Part 2

To be fair to Sergeant Jowls, he said next to nothing about my driving. The roads were icy, as was expected, but we spent just as much time out of the car as we did inside it. Payday Fridays usually started on a Thursday and would stretch across the whole weekend, until sometime through the day on Monday. Like many residents in Nuuk, I had often been late for work because of waiting for a bus that never came on a Monday morning, the driver having enjoyed far too much of the weekend.

That Friday night, driving with Jowls, was no different.

The first call was a minor scuffle, involving just three people. We got the second call of a disturbance while driving one particularly fiery middle-aged woman to the Greenlandic equivalent of a New York drunk tank. Jowls sent me back out alone while he and the duty officer processed the woman. I sped through the less populated streets, before slowing at the junctions, and then crawling along Nuuk's main street looking for Atii and Gaba who were dealing with a fight outside Nuuk's main watering hole: *Tupilaq*, or *Tupi* as most people called it.

I felt like I was cruising for trouble as I stared through the rain-splashed windshield, peering over the wheel and squinting into the swirl of blue emergency lights reflecting off the windows of the Thai restaurant, just down the street from the bar. But then I saw Atii, as she spilled into the street with a large man clinging to her back.

The tyres of the patrol car squealed along the kerb as I turned off the engine and yanked the handbrake into position. Atii had managed to roll out from beneath the man by the time I reached her, but only just. The rain that had plastered Atii's hair to her forehead now did the same to mine, and I felt a shiver down my neck as my skin cooled in the wind. The man stumbled to his feet, reaching for Atii, until I got a grip of his wrist, bending it backwards just enough to turn the man away from the road, away from Atii, and back onto the pavement. He lashed out with his foot, and I caught the toe of his shoe on my shin, but not enough to push me off balance. Atii grabbed the man's other arm, and we *helped* him to the back of the patrol car, stuffing him into the rear while he kicked and spat.

The odour of old hops and yeast washed over us as he burped, threatening to unload the last few beers he had consumed. I risked a quick look at Atii before we pushed the man's boot inside the door and slammed it shut.

"Weren't we supposed to try and talk him down first?" I said, as Atii leaned against the rear door to catch her breath.

"I tried that, already," she said, wiping the rain from her face. "He was less than cooperative, to put it mildly."

"And where's Gaba?"

Atii pointed up the street. "Outside *Tupi*. With everyone else. This one," she said, tapping her finger on the glass of the door, "decided to make a run for it. I would have let him go, but Gaba told me to go get him. Something about him being a repeat offender, and the fact that he started the fight at the bar."

"So, you decided to impress Gaba, eh?"

"Don't start, P," Atii said, waving her finger.

She had that look, the one with the single arched eyebrow. I had teased her many times about how her eyebrow was hooked to the corner of her mouth, scrunching her nose as her mouth stretched to the right. It was a difficult look to mimic, but I tried my best, and nine times out of ten, it made Atii smile. But maybe she was tired that night, or I had hit a little too close to home. Regardless, the look that I loved so much faded as she nodded back up the street.

"We'd better get going," she said.

"Shall I take this one back to the station?"

I was getting used to the taxi run. Besides, not speaking Greenlandic had its advantages on Friday nights. I was often the designated driver, and I didn't mind the monotony of driving to the station and back.

"Sure," Atii said. "I'll see you in a while."

I watched her walk a short distance up the hill before climbing in behind the wheel. The drunk in the back was quieter than he had been on the street, and he changed tack as I started the car.

"I'm not a bad man, really," he said, switching

to Danish when he realised I didn't grasp Greenlandic.

"I understand," I said, as I pulled away from the kerb.

"You can let me go. I'm calm now."

"I'm sure you are."

It was a classic response, as if the trip to the station sobered some, though by no means all, of the Friday night drunks into startling moments of clarity. And some inspired ingenuity when searching for a way to avoid a night in jail.

"I could give you information," the man said. "I know things. And, if I told you them, you could let me go."

"It doesn't work like that," I said, as I turned down the street leading to the station.

The man fell silent, and I thought he had given up, but I soon discovered that he was wracking his beer-addled brain for just the right titbit of information that might get him out of the boot of my patrol car.

"I could tell you about the girl," he said. "The one they're looking for in the mountains."

I have to admit I slowed the car when he said that, parking on the side of the road before twisting the rear-view mirror to get a better look at him.

"Her name is Iiva Suersaq," he said. "And I know all about her."

Part 3

"You're not working a missing persons case," Jowls said, pointing at the drunk from my car as the man slumped in a plastic chair beside the duty officer's desk. "It's Friday night, Jensen. Did you forget? Or is your ego so big now that you think stopping fights on the street is beneath you?"

"That's not what I think," I said. "But they're still looking for her." I pointed at the television screen on the wall. "If he knows something about her…"

"We'll pass it on. When we have time, Constable Jensen." Jowls stabbed his finger at the door, and said, "You're needed back on the street."

I thought of several responses, but bit my tongue, hard enough to taste blood, and then stormed out of the station, back into the rain.

Jowls wasn't wrong, but I knew that the idea of a lowly constable having a desk and a phone gnawed at him. I was supposed to be fresh out of the academy – which I was. But *my* understanding of police work included using a high degree of initiative. We were supposed to think and consider our actions, *before* acting. Sometimes we had to think fast. But it seemed to me that every time *I* started to think, Duneq was there to put me in my place.

Of course, it could have been jealousy. Like many close-knit cultures, we Greenlanders were not immune to that. It could also have been because I was a woman, younger than him, at the very start of my career. I opened the patrol car door, frowning as a sympathetic thought fractured my mood. I batted the thought away – I wasn't ready to take Sergeant Duneq's side, or to see it from his perspective. Slamming the door helped. As did throwing the police car into gear, roaring out of the parking lot, and spinning into the street.

I was too focused on trying to remain angry to notice the black skin of ice lining the road.

The minute I left the gravel surface of the police parking lot, the rear end of the patrol car settled onto the ice, spinning me around until I was facing the police station. The passenger side of the car bounced over the sand and grit lining the side of the road, catching me by surprise, and flooding my body with adrenalin, as I thought about the irrigation ditch running alongside the road. I'd like to say it was experience, or more of that quick thinking I was convinced a young police constable such as myself was capable of. Whatever it was guiding my foot to the accelerator, stomping on the pedal as I wrenched the steering wheel down to the left, it smelled a lot like luck to me. I hit the brakes as I pulled away from the ditch, skidding to a stop with one set of wheels on the grit and the other on the slick asphalt.

"Stupid," I said, casting a glance at the police station to see if anyone was watching.

I saw Sergeant Duneq leaning against the wall

beside the front door, his arms wrapped around his belly as he tucked fat thumbs into his low-hanging utility belt. The light from the entrance was strong enough to reveal the sneer on his face, and I could just imagine his voice, reminding me that *training was over.*

I wondered if it ever would be, and if that really was the point of it all, that we were always learning, that no two days were alike.

I checked the mirrors, breathed a sigh of relief that the only thing that had taken a hit was my pride, and then pulled away, turning slowly in the street. I headed back to the centre of Nuuk, cruising the streets for customers too rowdy for the average taxi. It didn't take long to find them, and I spent another two hours shuttling back and forth from the street to the station.

Back at the station, Jowls didn't say anything. Nor did he react as I checked the duty officer's list of guests in the cells, noting that Ulaajuk Corneliussen, my second customer that evening, was in cell three.

Part 4

Ulaajuk Corneliussen's story was similar to that of the men and women in the cells either side of him. Armed with little more than a superficial education, plagued by truancy – his own and his teachers', Ulaajuk had once clung to the belief that he could make a living as his father did, hunting and fishing. But when the reality of life in the concrete apartment blocks of Nuuk struck him, when it became clear that fishing and hunting for a living was little more than a sentimental dream, Ulaajuk found his escape in alcohol.

As sad as it was, there were so many Ulaajuks in Greenland, they created a stereotype that foreigners, and especially Danes, with that strange mix of post-colonial affection and disdain, found all too easy to believe. I knew that we had the same potential as the Danes and the Europeans among us, but that circumstance often prevented us from achieving the goals we set in our youth. Changing course required more than just willpower; a helping hand was often necessary, just to hold certain doors open, long enough to allow people like Ulaajuk to step through them.

And people like me, I thought, as I unlocked Ulaajuk's door.

The few hours' rest, some food and coffee, had

given Ulaajuk time to sober up. Enough, I hoped, to jog his memory about the girl. He stirred as I entered the cell, swinging his legs over the side of the bed as I sat down on the chair opposite him.

"You're staying the night," I said, as he looked up. "I'm not here to let you go."

"Okay," he said, He brushed his thick black fringe out of his eyes.

"I'm on a break. But I want to know about the girl."

"Iiva?"

"Yes."

Ulaajuk nodded. "She's a good girl. I hope they find her."

"You said you could tell me about her. Maybe what you tell me will help."

I resisted the urge to wrinkle my nose as Ulaajuk shifted on the bed. He might have sobered up, but the confines of the cell did nothing to dampen the heady mix of fart, beer and sweat. Ulaajuk rested his hands in his lap. With his legs stretched out on the bed, and his back against the wall, he reminded me of a hunter on his sledge, perhaps even a younger Tuukula. The thought made me smile, and I wondered what Tuukula and Luui would have said about my wild ride out of the parking lot. Ulaajuk brought me back to the present with a soft cough as he cleared his throat to speak.

"They say she has a raven tongue," he said, as I tugged my notebook out of my jacket pocket.

"Why?"

"Hair lip," Ulaajuk said, tapping his top lip. "She sounds funny when she speaks. The other children tease her."

"Funny?" I fought back a sudden wave of pity for Iiva. With my limited Greenlandic, I knew what it was like to have something children could make fun of. But pity wouldn't help me find her, when or perhaps *if* I was even given the chance.

"*Aap.*" Ulaajuk nodded. "It sounds like she speaks through her nose."

"Then why do they say she has a raven tongue?"

"Because she can talk like a raven – every sound."

I made a note, pausing with my pen on the paper as I thought about the range of raven calls that I had heard over the years. Such noisy brutes, they are so entangled in our daily lives it's difficult to imagine a Greenland without ravens. For the same reason, it can be difficult to think about them in a more abstract way. But as Ulaajuk told me about Iiva, I remembered my own childhood, how we used to try and mimic the ravens, calling them to us, only to have them dance away as we tried to catch them.

"Iiva found a raven nest once," Ulaajuk said. "She was five. The adults were gone, and she looked after the young." He scratched his head. "Two, I think."

"She reared them?"

"What?"

"She fed them," I said.

"*Aap.*"

"And they followed her around?"

"All over town." The dim light from the cell

lamp in the ceiling danced across Ulaajuk's dark brown eyes as if he was remembering another story about Iiva Suersaq and her ravens. "They used to sit on the school roof, opposite her class," he said, straightening his arm and shaping his hand like a beak.

He tucked one hand under his elbow, splaying his fingers like claws, and I imagined them gripping the edge of a roof. The memory of ravens hopping and scratching the bitumen roofs at the children's home brought a smile to my face as Ulaajuk continued.

"The teachers would send her out to shoo them away. But then she never came back. She would spend all day with them." The light in Ulaajuk's eyes faded as the raven evaporated. He returned his hands to his lap. "Her father, her *ataata*, hated the ravens."

"Why?"

"He wanted her to make friends, and to stay in school. He didn't believe the ravens could teach her anything." Ulaajuk dipped his head, resting his chin on his chest.

"Ulaajuk," I said. "How do you know Iiva?"

The light flickered as Ulaajuk looked up. I had the strangest feeling that he was drawing on the energy from the lamp, just as the light had made his eyes dance, now it seemed to lift him, giving him courage to say something – perhaps even to confess.

I waited for him to speak, lowering my notepad to my thigh. The chair creaked in the sudden silence of the cell.

"Iiva is my niece, my sister's daughter. I used

to look after her when I lived in Maniitsoq. Before I moved to Nuuk." The light flickered, surging, released from Ulaajuk's grasp.

"You think it's your fault that she ran away?"

I bit my lip as soon as I said it, wishing I had kept the thought to myself, wondering if I was fishing for a confession, as I imagined all kinds of scenarios where an uncle might have abused the trust of his sister, and taken advantage of Iiva. There was, unfortunately, plenty of documentation and many cases to support such a theory. But as I waited for Ulaajuk to respond, I realised there were just as many alternatives.

"*Aap*," he said, lifting his head. "I let her down."

"How?"

"Before I moved to Nuuk – a few years ago – she used to talk to me when her *anaana* was working, and she couldn't talk to her *ataata*."

"Why couldn't she talk to her father?"

Ulaajuk took a breath, and then said, "Because he hates ravens."

Part 5

"My dad's friend had a hair lip," Atii said, in my apartment after our shift had ended. She slumped in the chair opposite mine at the kitchen table. Breakfast, she had decided, should be at my place, and we agreed that everything in the fridge or the cupboards should be fried. It's amazing how the palate craves fat after working long dark hours, at least, that's what we told ourselves. After ploughing through fried bread, fried bacon and experimental granola – cornflakes not oats, there was little left to do but finish our coffee before crashing on the sofa with an episode or two of something, *anything*, before we returned to the station for the Saturday evening shift.

I reached over the table to twist a strand of Atii's hair out of her coffee and was rewarded with a tired smile, followed by a long sigh.

"He had surgery when he was a kid, but he still talked funny," she said. And then, "I think they call it a *cleft* lip now."

"And people need surgery?"

"*Aap*," she said. "I'm pretty sure. Something about eating, breathing, and talking. All of which is difficult with a hole in your palate." Atii paused to stick her finger in her mouth, frowning as she poked around the roof of her mouth. "God, I'm tired," she said, wiping her finger on her trousers. "What are we watching?"

"*Friends* or…"

"*Friends*," Atii said. "That's about all I can manage."

I finished my coffee as Atii drifted from the kitchen to the sofa. The cushions sighed as she flopped onto them. She hooked one stockinged foot over the back of the sofa as she rummaged around for the remote.

"On the coffee table," I said, as my phone rang.

"Tell them you're not home," Atii said. She flicked the television on, then reached for the second remote to turn on the DVD player.

"It's Jowls," I said, suppressing a sigh as I answered my phone.

My sympathetic gene, the one I suppressed earlier in my shift, engaged as I listened to Sergeant Duneq. He sounded even more tired than Atii. But as soon as I realised the direction in which the call was heading, I wished I'd never answered it.

"What?" Atii said, as I stuffed my phone into my pocket. She muted the *Friends* introduction and waited for me to speak.

"He wants me to go in."

"Now? You've only just got off."

"Someone called in sick."

"So? You've just done a night shift."

"He said there's no one else."

"Then let *him* do it."

As tempting as it was, I knew I would go in. My mind was already in the hall, waiting for my body to catch up, to slip into my jacket and pull on my boots.

"It's just a few hours. He's got someone coming in at noon."

"Noon? What about our morning together?"

"You'll be asleep before the opening credits," I said, tucking my hair behind my ear as I nodded at the television. "You always are."

"That's hardly the point, P."

"I know, but that's the way it is." I leaned over the back of the sofa to kiss Atii's head, then plucked the remote from her hand to toss it onto the armchair by the balcony door. "If you want sound…" I said, waiting for a response.

Atii rolled onto her side, hugging the pillow to her chest as she settled into the sofa. "I've seen this one before."

"Atii," I said, as I walked down the short corridor to the front door. "We've seen them *all* before."

"Right."

"I'll catch you later."

"At noon?"

"*Imaqa*. Maybe."

"Gaba has invited me to lunch."

"What?" I paused; fingers clasped around my jacket zip. "You never said."

"You never asked."

"I guess I didn't."

I shouted goodbye as I left my apartment, wishing her luck and reminding her to behave. I waited for a response before closing my door, but all I could hear were Atii's soft snores drifting down the hall.

Jowls sent a patrol car to pick me, making me think he wasn't all bad, and I clambered into the passenger seat. Constable Kuno Smidt grinned as he pressed a cup of takeaway coffee into my hands.

"Thought you might need this," he said, as I settled into my seat.

"You're a lifesaver, Kuno."

"You say that now but wait 'til we get to the station."

"What's going on?"

"Duneq is all fired up over something."

"Something about me?"

"You could say that." Kuno braked for a stop sign, resting his elbow on the side of the door, and tapping his fingers against his bald head. From a certain angle he reminded me of Gaba, and I wondered if Kuno was losing his hair, or borrowing the look from the SRU leader. He accelerated once the traffic started to move, then slowed for a bus to pull away from the kerb. The rain glistened on the granite lumps that rose like black pyramids behind the new high rises lining the road out of Qinngorput. "It's your phone," he said, as he settled in behind the bus. "It's been ringing all morning."

"My phone?" I said, blinking my way out of drowsiness and back into the conversation.

"The one on the missing persons desk."

"It's ringing?"

"Yes," Smidt said. He turned his head to smile. "You really are tired, aren't you?"

"Yes," I said. But the prospect of a missing persons case lit a small fire in my belly, and I felt its glow spread through my body. "I'll need more coffee," I said, and Smidt nodded.

Part 6

Sergeant Duneq was sitting on one end of my desk, looking just as tired as I felt, if not more so. His arms were folded stiffly on top of his stomach, as he scowled at Commissioner Lars Andersen. He turned his scowl towards me as I walked along one side of the long open office to the stairs at the far end. The Greenland missing persons desk – *my* desk – was stuffed beneath the stairs, in an area that Jowls dared me to call an office.

"I appreciate your concern," the commissioner said, nodding at me as I approached. "But this is a matter of national interest. It's already all over the news. The military need the Challenger jet on the east coast, and the politicians are claiming that we have given up the search. But the fact is, we have exhausted the possibilities. We have to show that we haven't given up, even after the search has been called off."

I caught a flash of something in the sergeant's eyes at the word *search*, and then the fuzziness of a late night shift, followed by an extra morning at work, cleared. Suddenly I realised they were talking about the missing girl.

"You mean they've stopped looking for Iiva Suersaq?" I said, drawing a look of wrath from Jowls, and a much softer and curious response from the commissioner.

"What do you know about her?" the commissioner asked.

"Only that she's eleven. She's been teased a lot – probably."

"Teased?"

"She has a cleft lip, and…" I paused, trying to remember what Atii had said. "A cleft palate – I think the two go together. Something that would make it hard for her to fit in." I was back in familiar territory and waking up, encouraged by the commissioner's nods of approval. "That might be a reason why she got lost in the first place," I said.

"You don't know that, Constable."

Jowls fixed me with a hard stare, raising his eyebrows, as if ordering me to stand down. But with the police commissioner standing right beside us, I was too excited to stand down. It was probably one of the reasons Sergeant Duneq made my life as miserable as possible. *Enthusiasm,* he had once told me, *was for intellectuals. But police work is practical work, Jensen. Remember that.*

I did remember. I remembered everything Jowls told me, if only to prove him wrong, every chance I got.

"Let her finish, George," the commissioner said.

Andersen took a more casual stance, resting his arm on top of a tall filing cabinet before gesturing for me to continue. I wasn't short, but the more time I spent with the commissioner, the shorter he made me feel. I took a breath, avoiding Jowls' renewed attempts to stare me into submission, and continued.

"If they've called off the search," I said, thinking on the spot. "That might suggest she's not lost but hiding."

"Or dead," Jowls said.

"I appreciate your optimism, Constable," the commissioner said, with a glare at Jowls. "But we're assuming the worst. It has been a wet and cold weekend. Plenty of ice in the foothills, more in the mountains. But," he said, with a wave of his hand. "Keep going. Elaborate."

"Okay," I said. "Supposing she's alive, then she might have a preferred hiding place, somewhere she's been before. It might be high up – higher than expected."

My desk creaked as Jowls shifted his weight. A deep crease of something like curiosity furrowed his brow as he leaned forwards. "What makes you say that?"

I shelved the realisation that he was curious, saving that thought for another time, as I scrabbled for an explanation.

"Because of the ravens," I said.

"Ravens?"

It was the commissioner's turn to frown.

"Yes. Her uncle told me she reared some orphan ravens."

"Orphan ravens?" Jowls snorted, and I paused, waiting for him to crack a comment about my orphan childhood. To his credit, and to my amazement, he didn't. Which only put me even more on the spot, as I searched for an explanation.

"She's been teased," I said.

Jowls snorted for a second time. "You've said

that already."

"Yes…"

"Go on, Constable," the commissioner said. "Never mind the sergeant. Tell me about the ravens and the girl's uncle."

"Her uncle, Ulaajuk, is in the cell downstairs."

"Was," Jowls said. "I let him go this morning."

"But before he went," I said, suppressing a sudden rush of urgency, and the thought that I might need to interview the girl's uncle again. "He said that Iiva spent lots of time with the ravens. They followed her around, and people shunned her even more because of that. Her cleft lip would have left a scar, and maybe a speech difficulty. It would have made her an easy target. Add the ravens to that and…" I paused as the duty officer knocked on the office door.

"Sergeant?" he said. "Can I have a word?"

The commissioner waited for Jowls to leave, then lifted his finger for me to hold any further thoughts I might have.

"The media is involved now, asking all kinds of questions about budgets and resources," he said, once Duneq and the duty officer had left the office. "Which means the politicians are obliged to comment. Now, I don't know much about the situation, only the basics. You've already told me more than I think anyone involved in the search knows. Which is why I'm sending you to Kangaamiut."

"Kangaamiut?"

"The village where Iiva Suersaq lives. Apparently, it was the old trading station, way back when, before they resettled in Maniitsoq." The commissioner laughed. "That's enough history for now."

"You're sending me today?" I barely heard the last part of what the commissioner said about history.

"Yes," he said, with a nod of his head. "I know you're tired, Constable."

I was, and yet, surprisingly, I was gaining strength as he spoke.

"I'm all right."

"Well," the commissioner smiled. "Let's pretend that you are. But let me make this clear. You will be seen as little more than a gesture. The family – the media too – will be expecting a renewed search. We simply don't have the resources, and the Challenger jet is unavailable. Between you and me, if the Challenger couldn't find her or even her body…"

"She might not want to be found," I said.

"Right. Which lends a little more credence to your theory. But, regardless of all that, this search, and this girl, suddenly got politicised. But nothing changes the fact that someone told the girl's mother that we now have a dedicated missing persons desk, and she called to ask for your help. Not by name," the commissioner said, as I started to speak. "But she might as well have. So, I'm sending you up the coast to look for Iiva. But I want you to understand that she is probably dead, and that really, your main task, is to confirm that, so we can close the case and allow the girl's parents to grieve." The commissioner paused for a second, dipping his head to look in my eyes. "Do you understand, Constable?"

"Yes."

"Good." He took a breath. "Now, with the limited resources available, and some funds I can scrape together, tell me what you think you might need. Bear in mind I can't give you any staff. I think Sergeant Duneq would have a stroke if I did," he said, and laughed.

"Yes, Sir," I said, as I thought about the girl, the reason she might be hiding, not lost. I thought about the ravens, and how she might be closer to nature than I was, and how the other children and adults shunned her for her strangeness. If she talked with the ravens, they might even think she had magical powers.

It was the thought of magic that did it.

"I do need some help," I said.

"And I said I can't spare any more officers."

"I know," I said. "But Tuukula isn't a police officer. He's a shaman."

Part 7

I rested my arms on the table in the airport waiting lounge in Nuuk, as I left a message on Atii's phone, wishing her luck with Gaba, before smiling at our different weekend *dates*. While Atii would be trying to keep her cool while staring at the muscle-bound Sergeant Alatak, leader of the Special Response Unit, with his shaved and oiled head and perfect pectorals… I had to stop myself at that point, as I found the image of Gaba's chest more than a little distracting. *Let Atii be distracted,* I thought, as a smile crept across my lips. I would be spending the rest of the weekend, and maybe longer, with a seventy-year-old magician and his five-year-old daughter. If I avoided all further thoughts of Gaba Alatak, and what he might be doing with my best friend, I found the anticipation of seeing Tuukula and Luui again to be more than compensation.

"Gaba invited Atii," I whispered to myself, as they called my flight. "Not me."

I tugged my daypack onto my shoulder as I stood up, slipped my phone inside my jacket pocket, and got in line for the flight. The passengers disembarked, filing down the steps of the De Havilland Dash 7, which was parked on the apron outside the lounge. I caught the familiar blue-black uniform of a police officer as he followed the other passengers to the baggage area, but no matter how hard I tried, I couldn't place him. It was silly to think that I could possibly know all the police officers in Greenland, but we were a relatively small group, supported by temporary officers from Denmark, like Kuno Smidt. Although, in Kuno's case, it was widely known that he was choosing longer and longer temporary positions. It was just a matter of time before he applied for a permanent one. But the police officer walking into the airport was new to me.

The passengers in front of me shuffled forwards as the door ahead of us opened. We filed into the baggage area, before showing our boarding cards at the gate. I caught the police officer's eye, and he grunted in return. The grunt did little to invite further conversation, and I let him be. Although, his deep brown skin, wispy oriental-style beard, and keen eyes intrigued me. He looked like he spent a lot of time outdoors. That thought brought me sharply back into the moment, and I sloughed off another bout of tiredness as I walked to the Dash 7, climbing on-board with no more thoughts about the police officer in the airport. The plane took off according to schedule, and I made myself comfortable, hoping to catch at least an hour's sleep between take-off and landing. When Jowls heard about my assignment and my final destination of Kangaamiut, he let a smile cross his face as he showed me the weather forecast on his phone just before I left the station, highlighting the strong winds with gleeful taps of his pudgy fingers.

"You'd better sleep on the flight, Jenson," he

had said. "Because the boat ride is going to be rough."

Maybe Jowls was right, but it didn't make any difference. I couldn't sleep, my brain was too awake for that. So, I said *yes* to coffee with plenty of sugar and cream. I made space for my cup on the table alongside my notebook and smartphone. Between texting Atii and checking my flight, I had time to find out more about cleft lips and palates, marking notes on my phone, before adding them to my notebook. I tucked my hair behind my ear as I worked, sucking at my top lip as I tried to imagine what services would be available to a family with a small child in need of speech therapy. *There would be something in Maniitsoq,* I thought, but I knew that the search had been in Kangaamiut, the mountainous coastal settlement where the girl lived. Getting to and from the town would be prohibitive enough, even in good weather, making it difficult to keep regular appointments.

The captain announced that we would be landing, adding a courteous reminder about the turbulence often encountered when landing in Maniitsoq – something about a right-angle turn on the approach. I stuffed my notebook and phone into my pockets, finished my coffee and readied myself for a bumpy landing.

The captain wasn't wrong. There was plenty of turbulence to make the approach to Maniitsoq *interesting*. But the turbulent landing was gentle, compared to Luui's welcome hug as she launched herself from Tuukula's arms and into mine.

"I've missed you too," I said, as Luui pressed

her face into my neck, and stuffed her cold fingers into the collar of my jacket. I stepped to one side to let the other passengers weave around me, the shaman, and his daughter.

"You're lucky we were close," Tuukula said.

"Where were you?"

"Visiting Luui's mother in Ilulissat." Tuukula smiled as a mischievous light flashed in his eyes. "So," he said, avoiding any further comment. "We are looking for a missing girl?"

"Yes," I said, tilting my head to one side as Luui played with my ponytail. "But we have to keep it quiet. That's why it's just you, me and Luui."

"We need to keep it quiet?" Tuukula frowned, and I smiled as his bushy grey eyebrows arced in thick curves beneath his thick grey hair. He wore the same tight bun on top of his head that I remembered from the first time we met in the far north of Greenland.

"It's complicated and political," I said, as Luui and I rubbed noses. She squirmed in my arms and I set her down, curious at how much she had grown in such a short space of time. "No media, so no interviews. We're here to help the family, and find the girl, as quietly as possible."

Tuukula dipped his head towards the door leading out of the airport and into a car park full of cars, as well as a small crowd of journalists and photographers.

It occurred to me that very few people knew I was going to Kangaamiut. I wondered who might have tipped off the press and immediately I thought of Jowls. It would be just like him to complicate things, even when we were supposed to be on the same side.

"Okay. This just got interesting."

Part 8

Unlike Denmark or other countries with a road or rail infrastructure, or cheaper and more regular flights, journalists' movements in Greenland are limited. Here there would often be a local representative of Greenland's national television and radio station *Kalaallit Nunaata Radioa*, ready to drop what they were doing to follow a story. Local journalists might be teachers, shopkeepers or postal workers, anyone with an interest in the news, or simply the best available person in the right place at the right time. The journalists waiting in a small gaggle outside the airport building in Maniitsoq fit all categories, including professional journalists from *Sermitsiaq* and one Danish newspaper. I stalled at the door, taking a breath as I wondered how best to navigate through the throng to the police patrol car idling at the far end of the parking area.

"Here," Tuukula said, as he lifted Luui into my arms. "I'll deal with this."

Luui said something in the Qaanaaq dialect of Greenlandic, and Tuukula responded with a soft brush of his lips on her cheek and a whisper in her ear.

"What did she say?" I asked.

"That she can walk. That she's not a baby

anymore." Tuukula shrugged. "I told her I agreed, but that you needed a cuddle. In which case, she said you could carry her all the way to the boat."

I had forgotten about the boat, but the thought of carrying Luui *all* the way made my arms sag before Tuukula had even opened the door. Luui wrapped her thin arms around my neck and I shifted my grip to support her bottom; her feet slapped at the sides of my backpack, as she wormed her toes into the straps as if they were stirrups. Tuukula opened the door and led the way.

It might have been a small group of journalists, but they were tenacious, reflecting the local and national interest in the fate of the missing girl, and the reasons why the search had been called off. I dodged one microphone, and then slipped behind Tuukula. I blinked once in the flash of a camera, and then paused as Tuukula seemed to grow taller, right in front of me.

"Magic," Luui whispered in my ear, fiddling her tongue around the English word.

I was taller than Tuukula. I mean I *was* taller than him. But without a word, in any language, Tuukula seemed to anticipate each of the journalists' steps, as if he knew where they were going before they did. When a woman tried to take a picture, Tuukula appeared in front of her, a beat before she lifted the camera. More than one journalist poked a microphone into his chest, then pulled back with an apology on their lips, as if they were suddenly struggling with spatial relations. It made me think of public *relations*, and how refreshing it would be to be able to dodge difficult questions. But Tuukula didn't dodge anything, he *anticipated* movement, and he did so all the way to the patrol car, parting the journalists and clearing a path.

"I'm sorry," the local constable said, as he opened the rear passenger door. "I thought it best to wait by the car."

"It's okay," I said, as Luui tumbled out of my arms and onto the back seat. I glanced at Tuukula, now normal size, as he walked around the car to get in the back beside his daughter.

"Jiihu Eliassen," the constable said, thrusting his hand forwards to greet me. He wore a lopsided grin beneath a thin moustache. "I'm to take you straight to the boat."

"I thought I might get briefed at the station," I said.

"No time. Not if you want to make the boat. Otherwise you have to wait three more days before you can sail to Kangaamiut." Eliassen grinned as he backed out of the parking space. "But it's going to be bumpy. Big waves today."

I looked out at the deep blue sea and the white caps crashing into and around the icebergs plying the waters off Maniitsoq.

"Tell me about the search," I said, as Eliassen pulled away from the airport.

"We searched for two days, on foot. We had the Challenger for a few hours on the second day." He poked his finger towards the roof, and I resisted the urge to look upwards. "We found nothing, and the Challenger saw nothing. Nothing on thermal. No heat signatures. Nothing."

"So, no body?" I said, lowering my voice as I caught a glimpse of Luui in the backseat, teasing her father with spider fingers crawling on his legs.

"Unless she drowned," Eliassen said, also whispering. "We should have found a trace of something, but all we found was a pair of her shoes."

"Shoes?"

"Sneakers – dirty and patched."

"And they were the shoes she was wearing, when she disappeared?"

"Ah, *that* I don't know," Eliassen said. He slowed to let a small delivery truck drive past before entering the docks and driving all the way to the boat's gangplank. He stopped the car and turned the engine off. Sea spray pattered the window as the car rocked gently in the wind. "The mother, Kilaala Suersaq, hasn't said much. She's too upset."

"And the father?"

"Saamoq? He hasn't said anything. But we had a call early this morning. He was seen going into the mountains. The neighbour said it looked like he was going hunting."

"He took a rifle?" Tuukula asked.

"*Aap.*"

Tuukula nodded once, and then settled back on the seat. Eliassen watched him for a moment, glanced at me, and then asked, "Are you some kind of consultant? A tracker, maybe?"

"*Naamik,*" Tuukula said. "I am *angakkoq*, a shaman."

"Right…" Eliassen nodded his head, slowly.

"Tuukula has helped me before," I said. "We

found a missing boy in Qaanaaq."

"And the girl?" Eliassen asked. "Shouldn't she be in school?"

"Luui is five years old," Tuukula said. "I'm home-schooling her."

"To be a shaman?" Eliassen suppressed a laugh.

Tuukula shook his head. "*Naamik*. Luui is already a shaman. I'm teaching her to be a good one."

I jumped at the sudden blast of the boat horn, recognising my cue to catch the boat before the conversation really started to get interesting.

"We have to go," I said, opening my door.

The wind curled around the edges, tugging the door out of my grasp, until I took a firmer grip of the handle. Luui hopped out of the car on the lee side of the wind, flapping her arms like wings as Tuukula grabbed a canvas holdall from the rear of the police car. I didn't remember him carrying it from the airport, and wondered if it was more magic, if he could just conjure things at will.

"I arrived early," he said, as I stared at the bag. "I met the constable then. He said he was waiting for you." Tuukula grinned and then nodded at the large blue-hulled boat. The ice-class passenger ferry was well-suited to Greenland's coastal waters, providing a lifeline for Greenlanders for whom the cost of flying was prohibitive. "But we shouldn't wait any longer."

"No," I said, as I looked at the gangplank. It shuddered in the wind. I rarely ever got seasick, but then I rarely ever sailed. I just hoped Tuukula had some kind of magic for nausea. I tucked the thought away for later as I followed the shaman and his daughter onto the boat to Kangaamiut.

Part 9

I divided my time on the boat between freezing on deck and warming up inside until the need to vomit sent me back to the railings. Tuukula, as I expected, weathered the storm better than most of the passengers, but spent his time looking after his two girls, as he now called us. I drank a little of the bottled water he gave me, and then more as he watched me, waiting for me to take more than just a swallow.

"It's just going to come back up anyway," I said, shouting into the wind between bouts of nausea.

The bow of the boat crashed into another wave, before dipping the port side into the quarter hatched sea, only to roll back to starboard. Luui clung to her father's chest, her little face squished into his shoulder as he whipped a cotton smock from his holdall into a makeshift harness, binding his daughter to his chest. He fished a bandana out of his pocket, and I wondered if he was going to attach himself to me, perhaps tying our wrists together with cotton handcuffs.

"For your mouth," he said, pressing the bandana into my hand.

Luui wretched, and Tuukula turned his back towards the railing, as Luui spilled the little she had left in her stomach over the railings, splashing a thin stream down her father's back.

"Two hours," Tuukula said to me, as he wiped Luui's mouth.

I didn't think I could last two minutes.

But, in a moment of calm, when the crazy path of the waves aligned and everything was still, if only for a second, I saw a beauty in the blue-black sea. There was something reassuring in its power. When I looked at the obsidian surface, it looked back – not a reflection, but deeper somehow, as if there were secrets below, waiting to be revealed at the right time, to the right people, but not until they were ready to comprehend them. I had little doubt that Tuukula knew many of the secrets of the deep, and that he was teaching Luui the easier ones already. But it seemed to me, in my nauseous state, that I was paying the price for urgency, in an effort to get to Kangaamiut as quickly as possible, when I should have waited for better weather.

In Greenland you are at the mercy of the waves, the wind, and the ice and sometimes it pays to wait, and in the waiting, wisdom is often revealed. But for the life of me, I couldn't fathom what wisdom I would find staring over the side of the boat into the black sea.

And then the wind picked up.

I grasped the rail and heaved once more, and, together, Luui and I splashed Tuukula's clothes, as he took care of us.

I lost track of time, but as the sun broke through the anvil clouds above, and the waves leaked their energy back into the sea, the village of Kangaamiut, with its red, and green and blue wooden houses, popped out of the brown and black granite mountains. The peaks were slick with rain, shrouded in mist, now sparkling with rainbow orbs caught in the sun's rays. The boat slowed and the motors settled into a steady rumble, pushing us forwards until the dock loomed and the passengers began to gather their things.

"Kangaamiut," Tuukula said, as he unwrapped Luui from his chest.

"We made it," I said.

Luui slid down her father's leg as he lowered her to the deck. She clung to his knee, resting her head on his thigh as the crew moored the boat alongside the dock. The wind played with Luui's hair, tickling her face with long black strands. I could feel it doing the same with my hair, and I stared through a swathe of loose black strands, too tired to tuck them away.

There was a small group of people on the dock, huddled like the journalists, but with a patient energy that suggested they had been waiting a long time, that they would wait even longer, if need be. I watched the group – all women – as the crew rattled the gangplank into position and we prepared to disembark. Tuukula gestured for me to go on ahead, and as I walked down the gangplank, the group of women shuffled towards it, breaking the tiny circle to reveal another woman within. Never had I seen a more fragile soul, and, when she took my hands, her fragility seeped into my pores and I pulled her into my arms.

"My name is Petra," I said. "I've come to find

your daughter."

Part 10

Even though I am a part of Greenland and Greenland is a part of me, I am constantly reminded that it is the simple things that can have the greatest impact on people's lives. Perhaps it is the nature of life in Greenland. Even with the comforts that modern life provides, we are still living on borrowed land. Not borrowed from another people, but borrowed from nature, from the elements, at the mercy and whim of all those forces we simply can't control. We don't even try. It will be the visitors you see at the airport desk asking about the delayed flight, while the Greenlanders simply look out of the window, checking the weather, before returning to their iPads, their phones or just waiting, quietly, patiently.

Kilaala Suersaq had been waiting for word of her daughter for two long days. Hers was a forced patience. Helped and supported by her family and friends, Kilaala could do nothing but wait. And judging by the looks of her straggled hair, her bloodshot eyes, and the sniff that could have been a summer cold, but wasn't, Kilaala's patience had taken a toll on her mind and her body.

I was, perhaps, too quick to say I had come to find her daughter, and a quick glance at Tuukula confirmed it. But the act of coming to Kangaamiut, of making the effort – even though it was my job – seemed to lift her a little, and my words tumbled out before I could think through the consequences.

"I'll find her," I said, as Kilaala squeezed me so tightly I struggled for breath.

It was Luui who came to my rescue, plucking at Kilaala's jeans, waiting to be introduced. Even at five years old, it seemed that the shaman's daughter understood people. She understood what they needed. Kilaala's tears welled out of her eyes as she bent down to greet Luui, taking the little girl in her arms, as Tuukula introduced himself to Kilaala's friends. I caught the names but struggled with the comments they made in Greenlandic. Tuukula whispered a translation as Kilaala took Luui's hand and led us back along the dock and into the village.

"It's been tough," he said. "The women told me that Kilaala has not slept, that she can't sleep. Not until Iiva comes home."

"I said I would find her, Tuukula."

"*Aap.*"

"I spoke too soon. What if we can't find her?"

The probability of succeeding where a coordinated search from the land and the air had failed, was slim, but the commissioner believed sending me to Kangaamiut was the right thing to do, regardless of the result. The police did not have infinite resources. They were already stretched thinly across Greenland's vast and challenging geography, but it didn't take much to bring hope to those who had none.

It might be a small gesture, but it was something. It was a start.

"If we don't find Iiva," Tuukula said. "Then we will help her mother to grieve, so that Iiva will live on in her memory."

"And Iiva's father? What about him?"

I thought about Saamoq taking his rifle into the mountains. He wouldn't be the first Greenlander, overcome by grief, to choose a more drastic way to ease his pain. I worried that our search for Iiva might end with more than one missing person.

"I don't know," Tuukula said. "I will know more when we visit the house."

We didn't have to wait long. Luui stopped on the road next to a short rocky path leading to the door of a wooden house painted blue. The paint was fresh and had yet to be ravaged by summer winds loaded with sand, or the winter winds with sharp frosty breath. Luui scuffed her feet in the grit on the road as Kilaala said goodbye to the women who had followed her home. It seemed that we had replaced them, that now it was up to us to help Kilaala through the next stage of the search for her daughter. I took Luui's hand at the start of the path and followed her into Kilaala's home.

Kilaala chattered as we removed our shoes. I dumped my daypack on top of Tuukula's holdall and followed Luui into the lounge. The walls, like many homes in Greenland were plastered with photographs, most of them framed, some tucked into the corners of bigger frames, or tacked to the wall. The outer wall of Kilaala's lounge reminded me of a detective's notice board, the kind I'd seen in the movies or on television. There must have been over fifty photographs on the wall, and I took a moment to study them, as Kilaala made tea and coffee, with the promise of something sweeter for Luui.

Most of the photographs were of Iiva, and I recognised the one they had used on the national news when reporting the developments of the search. Iiva and Luui shared some similarities, not least their round cheeks. But Iiva's lip captured my attention, and a series of photos showed the progression from an angry red groove and stitches, to a softer white scar that divided her top lip. Iiva smiled in almost every photograph, even those taken shortly after her operation, when she was smaller than Luui.

I turned as Kilaala rattled a tray of mugs and a plate of raisin bread into the living room, sliding it onto the table before she joined me at the wall of photographs. Kilaala pointed at each one in turn, talking me through Iiva's childhood with a little help from Tuukula.

"Always happy," he said, nodding as Kilaala added more detail here, pointing at another photograph there. "Always smiling, even when she couldn't."

"Her eyes," Kilaala said, in Danish, and I knew exactly what she meant.

Iiva's eyes shone in almost every single photograph, even those that were wrinkled and torn – saved, perhaps, from enthusiastic and loving fingers.

"And this one?" I asked, pointing at the only photograph in which Iiva looked sad.

She was holding something dark in her hands,

pressed against the wrinkles of her stripey t-shirt. The contrast made it difficult to see, and I waited for Tuukula to translate Kilaala's words. He nodded as she spoke, and again when she finished.

"That was the day Iiva found the dead ravens," he said. "The adults had died, leaving the orphans she found in the nest."

"I know about them," I said, as I recalled what Ulaajuk told me back in the cell in Nuuk.

"There is more to tell," Tuukula said, as Kilaala gestured for us to join her at the table.

Part 11

Tuukula took a sip of coffee before settling into the role of translator. Kilaala sat down on the side of the table opposite the window, giving me the impression that she wanted to be able to see outside, to see the road and the people passing the house, just in case one of them was Iiva. I pushed back my chair as Luui clambered into my lap. She really was heavier than I remembered, and I caught Kilaala's eye as Luui made herself comfortable. Kilaala gave me a knowing look, together with a smile that I imagined might be shared between mothers all over Greenland. Tuukula shook his head, ever so slightly, but enough to catch my attention, suggesting that this was not the time to ruin the illusion. So, for the remainder of our time in Kangaamiut, or at least the time we spent at the table, Luui was my daughter. I fussed with Luui's hair as Kilaala started to talk, pausing every now and again for Tuukula to translate.

"It was the winter she turned five," Tuukula said, as Kilaala dipped a cube of sugar into her coffee and sucked at it. "Iiva found a raven's nest on a path running above the last line of houses." Tuukula added something in Greenlandic, and Kilaala nodded as he pointed to the north and east. "She was with her mother," he said. "And Kilaala helped her carry the two raven chicks home."

"Saamoq doesn't like ravens," Kilaala said in Danish.

I could only imagine why.

Ravens are the ubiquitous bird of the north, staying year-round, through the long summers and dark winters. They are hardy and wily, and I remembered seeing ravens on the streetlights one autumn, when it was still too light to trigger the bulbs, but cold enough for snow and freezing temperatures. More than once, I thought I saw the big black birds covering the lamps with their wings to fool the lights into thinking it was darker than it was, turning on the lights and drawing heat from the bulbs.

Hardy and wily.

"And noisy," Tuukula said, as Kilaala continued her story. "Iiva hid the orphan ravens in the shed, feeding them fish from Saamoq's drying racks, and flakes of dry whale meat."

Tuukula smiled at the thought, and I pictured his drying racks on the beach in Qaanaaq, the very north of Greenland. That thought led to another, and suddenly I was on the sledge heading north, until Luui tapped my thigh and I realised that, still tired, my mind had wandered. I tuned into Kilaala's story at the moment her husband discovered the ravens.

"Saamoq was angry," Tuukula said. "The ravens had shit everywhere and had plucked the stitches from his sealskins." He laughed, and I imagined that the thought of ravens getting inside a hunter's shed was unthinkable. "Saamoq found Iiva on the floor of the shed talking to the ravens."

"How?" I asked, remembering to look at Kilaala.

Tuukula waited for Kilaala to speak before answering for her. "She mimicked the noises they made, the cawing, the shrieking and that…" He paused, searching for the words in Danish.

"The water drop," I said, frowning for lack of a better way to describe it. Everybody knew what it was, we had all heard it. But even as children we struggled to emulate it. It was as if the raven could drop the note from its throat to its toes, echoing dully on the way down.

"*Aap*," Tuukula said. "Iiva spent all her time in the shed for a week, and then, after Saamoq turfed the ravens into the snow, she would sit on the deck, with the ravens on the railings. Iiva fed them and they talked to her. She made the same noises that she'd learned from the ravens."

"And that was the first time she spoke," Kilaala said.

"What?"

"Iiva had an operation to seal the hole in her palate and to close her lip before she was eight months old," Tuukula said, pausing as Kilaala explained. "When she was older she could only make sounds. She struggled to say whole words, as if she couldn't get her tongue around them."

I was tempted to pull out my notebook, to recall what I had read of the hole in the palate of a child with a cleft palate, and how the air – and food – would escape up the child's nose. Eating and speaking were difficult. They were skills that had to be learned and practised. If Iiva had been in

Maniitsoq, she might have had a speech therapist. She would definitely have had one in Nuuk. But in Kangaamiut? I wondered.

Both Tuukula and Kilaala were quiet, waiting for me to return from my thoughts.

"Sorry," I said. "I was wondering if Iiva had a speech therapist. Someone to help her."

Kilaala spoke and Tuukula nodded, creasing his lips in a knowing smile.

"She had the ravens," he said.

"Saamoq," Kilaala said, pausing as she framed her words in Greenlandic, before trying them again in her halting Danish. "He said she had a raven tongue."

Tuukula smiled again, glancing at Luui, raising his eyebrows at the thought of Iiva talking with ravens when she was just five years old.

"*Naamik*," Kilaala said. "It was not good."

"Why?" I asked.

I had to wait as Kilaala struggled through a long explanation, one which flattened Tuukula's smile, and revealed a deeper pain that Kilaala carried. It seemed the thing that helped her daughter the most, was the very thing to drive Iiva and her father apart.

"He hates ravens," Kilaala said.

"Why?"

"Scavengers and thieves," Tuukula said. "That's what he called them." He paused again when Kilaala spoke, before adding, "He didn't want his daughter to learn the language of thieves, and he shooed them away."

Luui turned in my lap as Kilaala left the table to pluck a photograph from the wall. She returned to the table, pausing by my side to slide the photograph in front of me. She brushed a tear from her cheek, but not before one fell onto the photograph, glistening in the spring light shining through the window.

"He killed one of them," Tuukula said, repeating it in Greenlandic.

Kilaala sniffed once as she nodded, and then sat down.

Luui shifted in my lap to get a closer look at the photograph. She gently wiped Kilaala's tears from Iiva's cheeks with her tiny thumbs, and then cawed, just once, as ravens do.

The raven tongue was the language of thieves, according to Iiva's father. It made me wonder if Iiva had indeed gone missing, lost in the mountains, or if she had been stolen.

"And then," Tuukula said, as he translated. "Just a few days ago, Iiva found another nest."

Part 12

Ravens are survivors. And, with Iiva's help, according to Kilaala, Iiva had been determined to help the new raven young to survive, even if it meant hiding them from her father.

There were ravens in the mountains around Qinngorput, the area where I lived in Nuuk. They flew down the steep walls of black granite, the same walls that revealed winter's progress as it crept down the mountain to the east of the apartment blocks, the store, and the school. But unlike Nuuk, the houses of Kangaamiut were built on the mountainside, staggered from the sea, as if one day, far into the future, they might stretch all the way to the summit.

Thinking about survival and thinking about life in a remote Arctic village, perched on the cliffs, just a stone's throw from the black Greenland seas, I wondered just how different the Greenlanders were from the ravens. Neither human nor bird flew south for the winter. They weathered the same storms as the Greenlanders did, sheltering between the same rocks, at the mercy of the weather systems curling around the same mountain peaks. Surely Saamoq should have understood, perhaps even embraced his daughter's connection with the ravens.

"You don't understand," Tuukula said, as he sat on a rock on the path, smoking his roll-up cigarette until the burning tobacco flaked at his fingertip.

"What don't I understand?"

"The effort it takes to catch the fish, to land the whale. How hard it is for Saamoq to provide for his family."

I had heard it before, but this time, with Kilaala's tears and the much loved and wrinkled photograph of her daughter fresh in my memory, I wasn't interested in defending Saamoq Suersaq.

Not in the slightest.

"He took away the one thing that was helping his daughter."

"The ravens followed her to school, Petra. Think on that," Tuukula said.

"One of them did," I said. "He killed the other one – one of the first ones. Remember?"

"*Aap*." Tuukula finished his cigarette. He plucked another from behind his ear, shrugging when I stared at him. "I'm travelling," he said. "I'm allowed two cigarettes a day."

"I don't care how much you smoke," I said. "I'm worried about Iiva."

"And her *ataata*," Tuukula said. "You should worry about him too."

I *was* worried about him. I looked up and along the path, wrinkling my nose in the thin cloud of smoke from Tuukula's cigarette, as I pictured Saamoq wandering the mountains, searching for his daughter, or perhaps searching for a place to die.

"Then think of Saamoq and his daughter," Tuukula continued. "He is powerless to help her. At least, from his own way of thinking." Tuukula paused to look up the path to where Luui was channelling a stream of meltwater with lichen-covered rocks and handfuls of pebbles. "He understands he must provide for his daughter. It's the only thing he can do – putting meat on their table, selling the rest. But he can't talk to her – at least he feels that she cannot talk to him. He leaves her alone, for that reason. Meanwhile, he struggles to repair his hunting gear. He must keep a store of food for his dogs, covering the racks with nets to dry the fish in the wind ready for the summer. The nets keep the ravens away from the fish, but then he worries about the flies, when they arrive in the spring. So, he dries too much fish too soon, and the racks are heavy. The ravens are smart," Tuukula said, tapping his head with the stub of his shortened finger, the one he lost in a hunting accident. "They use their weight to tip a spar of wood. So Saamoq chases them away, hammering another spar with more nails." Tuukula took another drag on his cigarette, watching me as he puffed the smoke in a small cloud above his head. "And it goes on, every day." He paused at my questioning look. "You believe in the ravens? That they helped Iiva to speak?"

"If she tried to copy them, yes," I said. "Maybe."

"You think they helped train her muscles?"

"Like a speech therapist would teach her to do."

"Different sounds, needing different muscles. Lots of practice."

"And then Saamoq put an end to that."

"Because," Tuukula said, "his feelings towards ravens are different to hers."

"And he couldn't see it."

"We don't know what he saw or what he sees. To know that we have to find him."

"You mean we have to look for Saamoq before we can look for Iiva?"

Tuukula finished his second cigarette. "*Imaqa*. But what's that over there," he said, with a nod towards Luui waving from the top of a boulder further along the path. "Maybe she has found something."

I walked beside Tuukula in silence, wondering if I had said too much. It was all so frustrating. We needed a practical piece of evidence, something that could lead us to the next step, and the one after that, until the missing person was found. At least, those were my thoughts as I walked beside Tuukula on the path leading up and into the mountains of Kangaamiut. It was the shaman's daughter who found the first practical lead in the search for Iiva.

"Shoes?" I said, as I crouched beside a small pair of shoes on the path. They were too big for Luui – she had already tried them on – and too small for an adult or a teenager.

"They must be Iiva's," Tuukula said.

"You think so?"

"The original search team found another pair further up the mountain," he said. "You told me that."

"Yes, but wouldn't they have found this pair first, on the way up the path?"

"They should have, unless…"

I caught the quizzical look on Tuukula's face, and, in a sudden burst of light as the clouds evaporated in the sun, I saw my own reflection in his eyes – just as quizzical, equally curious.

"Unless," I said, "they were left here recently." I felt my brow wrinkle, just above my nose, the way Atii said it did when I was puzzling things out. "But then they could be anybody's."

Luui said something to her father, then clambered down the other side of the rock, leaping the last metre to land in a patch of refrozen snow, like a dune of hailstones. She called for us to come. As we rounded the boulder she lifted up a stripey t-shirt, pressing it against her chest as if trying it on. Unlike the shoes, the t-shirt was the right size, and I remembered another five-year-old girl who had one just like it.

"Iiva's," I said. "From the photograph."

"When she was five years old." Tuukula looked up, scanning the lower outcrops of rock rising up the steep sides of the mountain.

We found more of Iiva's old clothes just off the path – a pair of cotton trousers, and a thin summer hat, hanging from a cross of wood clinched between a small cairn of Greenland rocks.

"A scarecrow?" I said. "Like in a farmer's field."

"There are no crows in Greenland," Tuukula said, as he studied the wooden cross. He pressed a cracked thumbnail into the wood, then sniffed at the oil that seeped onto it. "Fish," he said. "And seal."

"Someone built a figure of stones and wood, and dressed it with Iiva's clothes," I said, as my frown deepened to a pinch. "To scare the ravens away?"

"Maybe not to scare them away," Tuukula said. "Maybe to attract them."

"That doesn't make any sense," I said.

"Not to us," Tuukula said.

He looked down and smiled as Luui took his hand. She flapped her free arm like a wing, and then cawed like a raven, the same sound over and over, in the way that Greenlandic children did, all over the country. Except, in Kangaamiut, there was one girl who knew all the sounds, the whole raven vocabulary.

"We should follow the path," I said.

"*Naamik*," Tuukula said. "They've already tried that. We should follow the clothes."

Part 13

Luui led the way, scrambling off the path before slipping over slick black rocks, bald of snow, melted in the sun. I gathered up Iiva's clothes, and then followed Tuukula as he beat a trail between the rocks, picking his way up the mountain after Luui. I wondered when her little legs would start to tire, and when I might get a break. But Luui possessed a hidden energy that seemed to lift her from one bald rock to the next. Tuukula called for her to slow down, but Luui just waved, jabbing her tiny fingers at the ravens scrabbling about the rocks above.

"She's ignoring me," Tuukula said during a brief pause. We both watched as Luui continued to climb. "We'll have to talk later."

Since meeting Tuukula and his young daughter, I had often wondered about his approach to parenting. Like the children of many Greenlandic families, Luui seemed to enjoy a lot of freedom, with few noticeable boundaries. The boundaries of my own childhood had been drawn by child psychologists and pedagogues, enforced by strict curfews and regular evaluations. I used to envy the other children at school, how they could stay out late, even in winter, when I was scolded for the slightest infractions. As for Luui, now high up on the mountainside, it seemed her only limit was the sky itself, and gravity, keeping her feet on the ground, not including her short leaps between the boulders.

A raven's cry caught my attention, and I scanned the sky – bright now that the sun had burned fully through the cloud. There were at least four ravens – two on the wing, one cawing and clacking along a ridge halfway up a sheer rock wall, and the fourth hopping closer and closer to Luui.

"*Ataata*," Luui shouted. And then, in Danish, "Hurry."

Luui pointed at the raven and we picked up the pace, slipping and sliding up steep banks of melted snow, pressing our palms on stubby black lichen when we fell. Luui called again, urging us onwards and upwards with shrill calls, not unlike those of the raven.

"I need a break," I said, as I dropped Iiva's shoes. I knelt on the snow, gathered Iiva's shoes into my arms, and then tried to stuff them into my jacket pockets. Tuukula called out for Luui to stop, swearing when she didn't.

"These past few years have been challenging," he said, as he sat on a rock beside me.

"The past *few* years?"

"*Aap*. All of them. And every year she's stronger, more curious."

"She's only five," I said.

"And I am seventy-one." Tuukula laughed. "She's my first and only child. Never again. No more."

"I must admit," I said. "I'm impressed you've come this far."

"Up the mountain?"

"With Luui. Without help, I mean."

Tuukula shrugged, and said, "I wouldn't be able to keep up, if I didn't use a little magic in between. Only, this last year…"

I looked at Tuukula as his words tapered into thoughts. "Magic?"

"Just a little," he said with a shrug. "I ask the spirits to make her drowsy when I'm tired. Most of the time they listen, and oblige, but lately…" Tuukula paused to laugh, and I caught a flash of what looked like admiration in his eyes. "Lately, when I talk to the spirits, Luui seems to make them a better offer. I should be pleased, and I am, but I'm also tired, Petra. My daughter wears me out."

"She wears both of us out," I said, as I succeeded in zipping half of each shoe into my pockets. I pushed myself onto my feet and reached out for Tuukula's hand. "Come on," I said. "We'd better catch her up."

Tuukula took my hand, and I smiled at the warm dry touch of his wrinkled skin. We took it in turns to lead, pulling each other across slippery patches of snow, hauling each other over boulders. The ravens cawed above us, and, when we reached a flat area big enough for a house, Luui welcomed us with a cry of her own.

"Hurry," she said, pointing at a large crack in the rock, slicing a deep granite gash into the mountain.

"Wait," Tuukula said, as Luui slipped onto her belly to squirm through the crack.

Tuukula ran forwards, finding his second wind

as his daughter poked her head and shoulders inside the mountain. I ran alongside him, skidding onto my knees and reaching for Luui's feet as she turned to one side, determined to crawl all the way into the crack. I held the heel of her shoe for a moment before she tugged it free of my grasp.

"Luui," Tuukula said, as he lay on the rocks to shout into the mountain. "You must come back." He spoke in Danish, and I wondered if he switched between languages depending upon the impression he was trying to make on Luui. The greatest impression of her disappearance, however, could be seen on Tuukula's face, as he slapped his palm on the rock.

"We'll never get in there," I said. "She'll have to come back herself."

Tuukula pressed his face into the crack. "It's too steep," he said. "If she goes any further in, she won't be able to crawl back by herself. She'll need a rope. *We* need a rope."

"And help," I said. "One of us has to go back."

Everything changed in that moment, when the search for one girl turned into a rescue for another. *And I brought her here,* I thought, as I wondered what might have made Luui clamber up the mountain and then dive through a hole in the rock. I heard the clack of raven claws on the rocks above me and looked up to stare into the beady black eye of a male. A moment passed, and I could feel a shallow wave of empathy for Iiva's father. I wanted to blame the raven for encouraging Luui to crawl into danger. But it was just a raven. At least, that's what I told myself, as I checked my smartphone, cursing at the lack of signal.

"You stay here," I said to Tuukula. "I'll get help."

"And a rope," he said, calling after me, as I started back down the mountain, slipping and sliding towards the path below.

Part 14

Running down the mountain was harder than climbing up it. I lost track of how many times I slipped, thudding the base of my palms into rocks, feeling the dull creep of pain that increased each time I broke my fall.

But I was making progress.

I covered the same distance we had climbed in half the time, including the time I spent on my butt. When I reached the path, I had to pause to check my surroundings. I found the wooden cross and turned away from it, running down the path towards the village. My hair clung to my forehead in strands and I brushed them away, tucking them behind my ear or just letting them fly behind me as I increased speed. I was hot in my jacket but loathe to slow down to remove it. Keeping a steady rhythm was the key, anticipating the dips and grooves in the path, leaping onto one smooth-topped boulder and then scanning, hoping – sometimes attaching a silent prayer – that there would be another boulder to leap onto. But each time I mouthed the prayer I was already airborne, flying along the path with Iiva's shoes half-zipped into my pockets and her stripey t-shirt tucked into my utility belt.

I approached a long bend in the path, giddy at the sight of the roofs of the first houses below. I picked up speed, jogging a list of priorities through my mind. There had to be a volunteer fire department. They would have the equipment needed to rescue Luui. Perhaps it was still attached to the quad bikes – if they had quad bikes – from when they were searching for Iiva Suersaq. A doctor would be ideal, but the village, like so many other villages and settlements in Greenland, would likely only have an untrained medical assistant, traditionally known as the village midwife. My own medical training would have to suffice, and I wondered just what I could expect, what injuries Luui might have sustained deep inside the mountain.

As I ran down the steep path I had no idea how far Luui might have gone into the mountain, or how hurt she might be. Nor did it matter, as I careened at full speed into a man walking up it.

The man fell into the old snow and tough Arctic grasses just off the path. I slid over his body, turning a complete cartwheel before shuddering to a full stop. Everything hurt more than I wanted to think about. I almost laughed at the jumble of my thoughts, the mix of pain and potential chastisement as I rolled onto my side to apologise to the man. But when I saw the rifle levelled at my chest and heard the click and clack of the bolt as the man jacked a bullet into the chamber, I wondered just how much I had hurt him.

"I'm so sorry," I said in Danish. "I didn't see you."

The man, about the same height as me, and taller than Tuukula, kept his gaze fixed on my middle, and I looked down to see Iiva's shoes poking out of my jacket pockets, and her t-shirt flapping in a gust of wind twisting dirt along the path.

"Those don't belong to you," the man said. "Where did you get them?"

"These shoes?" I tried to catch the man's eye but failed. "I believe they belong to Iiva Suersaq. She's the girl who went missing just a few days ago."

Of course, I guessed that he must know that, and not just because the whole village had been on the alert to find Iiva, but because this man was her father.

"You're Saamoq Suersaq," I said, taking a step forward. "Aren't you?"

"Don't come any closer," he said, waving the end of the rifle in my direction. He lifted his head, briefly, but just long enough to make eye contact.

"I'm a police officer," I said. "I'm looking for Iiva."

"You have her clothes."

"Yes. I found them on the path." I pointed up the mountain, curious to see if the man would look the same way. When he didn't, I wondered what he knew about the effigy on the path. "I found them by a wooden cross, stuck between a pile of rocks. Do you know about that? Saamoq?"

The man reacted when I said his name, flashing me a hard stare as he raised the rifle, tugging the stock into his shoulder as if he was about to fire.

"Saamoq," I said. "Listen, I'm a police officer. I'm here to help."

"You have Iiva's clothes."

"Yes," I said, teasing my fingers around Iiva's t-shirt. "Yes, I do."

"You should have left them where you found them. They are not meant for you."

"Are they for Iiva?" I asked, wondering if he knew where she was, or if he expected her to come to the path for her clothes, even her old ones. Then he pulled the trigger. The bullet slammed into the crusty snow just an arm's length to my right, and I decided any further questions could wait. I glanced over my shoulder and leaped further from the path to slide down a tongue of old snow and gritty ice, fumbling to pull my pistol from its holster, as Saamoq ran after me.

Part 15

My pistol slipped out of my hand as I slammed my ribs into an exposed head of granite. The impact knocked the air out of my lungs and I fought for breath as Saamoq slid down the snow towards me, into a sitting position with his hands around his rifle, the barrel pointed at my chest. I saw my pistol in a hollow of snow just below me, and I reached for it, only to pull back my hand as Saamoq fired for a second time. The shot echoed around the mountain walls until the old snow absorbed it.

"For God's sake, Saamoq," I yelled, as my initial fear twisted into frustration. "I'm a police officer. Put your gun down."

Maybe I was more pissed than frustrated, losing a grip on my professionalism as I slipped and scrabbled to my feet, brushing snow out of the creases around my trouser pockets, and fixing Saamoq with an angry look as he slid to a stop in front of me.

Planned or not, it seemed to work.

Saamoq lowered his rifle, before slinging it over his shoulder as he stood up.

"I know you're upset, Saamoq. I know you're looking for your daughter…"

I was ready to say more, but the words died on my lips as Saamoq dipped his chin to his chest and covered his eyes with his hands. He shook as he sobbed, silently, the tears welling beneath his palms, before dribbling in slow streams along his thumbs.

"It's my fault," he said, as he lifted his head. Saamoq wiped the tears from his cheeks, sniffing several times as he caught his breath. "But she brought more birds home. *Tulugaq* – ravens."

"I know," I said.

"I knew she would go into the mountains. I know she has a hiding place somewhere up here." Saamoq looked around, staring at the walls of granite."I just don't know where."

"And you didn't tell anybody? What about the people searching for her?" I thought about the Challenger jet, and how, if Iiva was hidden underground, if she was deep enough, even the thermal cameras wouldn't find her.

"What would I tell them? That I scared my daughter into the mountains?"

"Yes," I said. "Exactly that."

"And then what?" Saamoq's lip curled as his face twisted beneath heavy black brows. "What would they think? Would they think I had done something to her? That I might have hurt her? *Naamik*," he said, shaking his head. "I would never hurt her, but those ravens…"

I tensed as Saamoq's hand drifted towards his rifle.

"Tell me about Iiva," I said, pitching my voice between us, softer than the wind teasing our clothes, but loud enough, I hoped, to show him I was listening, that I wanted to hear his side of the story.

I spared a thought for Luui and Tuukula but resisted the urge to run to the village – any sudden movement might send Saamoq over the edge, an edge that he was barely clinging to.

"I'm not a bad man," he said. "But I'm not a good father." Saamoq lifted his head, drawing strength from his words. A confession of sorts. "Kilaala loved Iiva from before she was born. And I thought I did too. But then, when there were problems, and the doctors said Iiva would need surgery, that she would need help to breathe and to eat, and that later, she would need help to talk. It was too much. Life is hard enough without such things. I have seen it. Weakness is death. My daughter was born weak – weaker than normal. I thought she would die as a baby, and I prepared myself. I let her go when I should have loved her. But if I loved her, and she died, what then? What would I do? I had to be strong for Kilaala. She would be crushed when Iiva died. I believed it was only a matter of time."

Saamoq looked into my eyes, and I held his gaze, nodding ever so slightly, encouraging him to continue. As alien as it seemed, I could almost understand his reaction, how he prepared himself to cope with what he thought was inevitable. As heartless as it was, it almost made sense as a coping mechanism – survival at its most primal.

"She didn't die," Saamoq looked away, staring up at the mountains. "But I had already distanced myself. I was convinced she would still die, if not one day, then the next. And when she didn't the gap between us was too great. I saw her weakness as my weakness. Her scar on her lip reminded me every day. So I stopped looking. Her voice – those breathy words – reminded me how weak I was every time I heard her speak, so I stopped listening. It was my way – the only way. Until the ravens."

Saamoq turned back to me, and I almost started at the fire in his eyes.

"The ravens, those thieves, they stole my daughter from me. When she found that first nest – she was just five years old. She brought those ravens home. Then I couldn't ignore her. I couldn't ignore the screeching from the shed. So loud. Every time I heard those birds, I would shout and curse. I made my wife cry. I made her run away to the bedroom. But my daughter was already gone, hiding in the shed. Then, when the screeching got louder and louder, I went to the shed. There was so much screeching, I thought there were more ravens, not just two tiny birds. When I opened the shed, I saw Iiva with these birds in her hands, wearing that t-shirt." Saamoq sneered as he pointed at my belt. "Iiva was screeching like the ravens, louder and louder. I shouted at her to stop. I think it was the first time I ever talked *to* my daughter," Saamoq said, before clasping his hand to his mouth. He let his hand fall, drawing a thin stream of saliva with it as more tears welled in his eyes. "My first words to Iiva, the first time I ever really said anything to her, were curses and shouts. I was angry. It's no wonder she ran away."

"She's run away before?"

"*Aap*," he said. "She grabbed those birds when I tried to take them. And she ran away. She was gone the rest of the day. When she came back, when her mother finally got her into bed, plucking those damned birds from her arms, I took them." Saamoq shook his head slowly as he wrung his hands around imaginary necks. "I killed the first one, and I dropped its body into the snow outside the shed. I left it there as I hunted for the second one. I forgot about the dead one. And I never found its brother. I should have thrown the body away. When Iiva found it, I remember thinking I was pleased she saw it. And then her mother took that photo."

"I've seen it," I said, softly.

"Over the years, so many times, I've tried to rip that photo in two. But each time I put it back," he said, lifting his hand in front of him, as if tucking the photograph back into the corner of the frame, exactly as I had found it.

"And then Iiva found more ravens," I said. "Is that what happened?"

"Just the other day," Saamoq said, and nodded. "Another abandoned nest. She brought them home, and when I saw them, I got mad. I chased her out of the house, and she ran away. She was gone for more than a day, and Kilaala called the police." He paused to look at me, as if seeing my uniform for the first time. "I knew she would come back. But when they stopped searching, and Kilaala got so upset, I knew I had to find her."

"So you went into the mountains."

"*Aap*," he said, pointing at Iiva's shoes in my pockets and her t-shirt tucked into my belt. "I knew she wouldn't come if I called, so I decided to bring her to me." He shook his head, suppressing a laugh as if the thought of what he did embarrassed him. "People say I'm crazy, and maybe they're right. But I know ravens," he said, jabbing his finger in the air between us. Then he tapped his forehead, and said, "I know how they think. They're curious. They are drawn to my daughter – she calls to them with her raven tongue. They know her clothes, her smell. So I made an Iiva. I made my daughter – stone dolls with her clothes, her smell, in different places in the mountains. You found one. I made more. Then when the ravens came, I shot at them, killing some before they got smart and left the dolls alone. Then I realised how stupid I had been. I thought if the ravens came, then so would Iiva. And now that I have taught the ravens to fear my daughter, they will never come to her, and I will never find her. She is gone."

Part 16

The snow crunched and squeaked as Saamoq sank to his knees in front of me. His rifle slipped from his shoulder and I took it, slinging it across my chest before reaching down into the hollow for my pistol. I watched Saamoq struggle in the wake of his confession as I holstered my pistol and snapped the cover closed. I pulled my smartphone from my pocket and sighed at the sight of three bars of signal. Constable Jiihu Eliassen answered my call from the station in Maniitsoq after just two rings, promising to contact the local volunteer fire chief as soon as I hung up.

"We have to go, Saamoq," I said, slipping my phone back into my pocket.

"Where?"

"There's a little girl who needs our help."

"Iiva?"

I shook my head. "My friend and his daughter."

Saamoq's story had given me some hope that maybe Iiva wasn't that far away after all. "If you help me help my friends, then I promise I won't leave Kangaamiut until we have found Iiva."

We picked our way across the snow to the path to begin our climb back up the mountain. I heard the chatter of small engines and smiled as I realised the volunteer fire department did have quad bikes.

Saamoq and I stepped to one side of the path as they approached.

"Up there," I said. "There's a crack in a rock."

"We know it," the fire chief said.

"You'll have to go on foot," I said.

"Not if we follow the path. It curves around the top and comes back down to that boulder."

"Boulder? I thought it was part of the mountain."

"*Aap*," he said. "It sheared off the mountain a long time ago. It's a boulder now."

I saw the frown on the fire chief's face, as if he was wondering why they hadn't looked there earlier, during the search for Iiva.

"It's okay," I said. "You were never going to find Iiva. Not if she didn't want to be found."

"Who crawled beneath the boulder?"

"Her name is Luui." I fought back a smile as I said her name. "And I have a feeling she is about to surprise us all."

The feeling grew stronger with every step we took along the path.

The three men from the volunteer fire department raced up the path, ploughing into the snow to curve around the larger boulders where possible. By the time we arrived at the boulder, they were rigging ropes and anchors in anticipation of crawling into the crack in the rock.

"They're too big," Tuukula said, as Saamoq and I approached. "I offered to go, but they told me I'm too old." He paused to look at Saamoq, nodding once before turning back to me. "I said you would go."

"Me?"

"You're taller than me, but slimmer than anyone here."

At any other time, it might have been a complement, but the practical aspect of rescuing Luui, kept me focused, and without another word I started to unbuckle my utility belt.

"Wait."

I looked up as the fire chief held up his hand, clicking his fingers to get our attention.

"What is it?"

"We heard something."

"Luui?" Tuukula asked.

"That's your little girl?" The fire chief nodded. "*Aap*, it could have been her. Come," he said, beckoning Tuukula closer to the crack in the rock. I knelt beside the shaman as he pressed his face beneath the boulder, as far as he could.

"Luui?"

"*Ataata*," Luui shouted back, bringing a smile to all our faces.

Tuukula said something in Greenlandic, before translating for me. "I said we have a rope." He paused, as Luui replied. "But she says she doesn't need it. She says there's a way out."

Tuukula pulled his head out of the crack and stood up. He pointed to the left, then jogged along the side of the boulder. I fastened my belt and followed, with Saamoq and the fire crew right behind me.

We heard the two girls a moment before we saw them, catching a flash of black feathers as Iiva released a young raven from her hands into the wind. I caught my breath, trying to stem a sudden rush of emotion as I looked at her. I failed, and the tears trickled down my cheeks as the two girls walked towards us, hand in hand, taking it in turns to call to the ravens above them.

"Iiva," Saamoq said, sinking to his knees as she stopped, hesitating, until Luul gripped her hand and tugged her around the last few rocks and into her father's arms.

"Magic," Luui said, pointing at Iiva wrapped in her father's embrace.

"*Aap*," Tuukula said. He knelt down to brush at the dirt on Luui's cheeks, licking his thumbs to rub at the stubborn patches, revealing her freckles and releasing a bout of giggles that reverberated around the rocks.

I stepped around the shaman and his daughter for a better look at Iiva. It was her eyes that caught me, as they burned with a new energy, hope, perhaps, for the future. She was taller than Luui, older by six years, but both girls possessed the strength and will power to make the impossible happen.

"Thank you," Iiva said, in Danish, with an almost imperceptible nasal inflection.

"You're very welcome," I said.

The fire chief tapped me on the shoulder, before nodding at Iiva and Saamoq. "We'll help them down the mountain, then come back for you."

"It's okay," I said. "I'd like to walk."

Tuukula nodded that he and Luui would do the same. We waited for Iiva and her father to climb onto the quad bikes. Luui waved as they pulled away.

"Now, Luui," Tuukula said, as he pulled his daughter into his arms. "We have to have a little talk."

Luui pressed her fingers to his lips, pinching them shut as she shook her head.

"Magic," I said, as I led the way back to the path.

Part 17

The fire chief had arranged mattresses and bedding on the first floor of the garage housing the gear and quad bikes. Luui swapped her raven shrieks for the shriek of a motorbike as she steered one of the stationary quads on an imaginary journey. Tuukula smoked outside, while I clambered up the stairs and flopped onto the nearest mattress.

I don't remember waking to eat, although Tuukula assured me that I did.

I vaguely remember lots of chattering, and the bounce of small bodies from one mattress to the next, but anything else is nothing more than a sleepy blur.

"You had a long talk with Kilaala," Tuukula said, as we sat at a table inside the boat on the way back to Maniitsoq.

"I did?"

"*Aap*," he said. "She told everybody what you said, that you would find her daughter. And you did."

"Luui did," I said.

"She played her part. We all did."

Tuukula fiddled with a tin of tobacco, rolling two cigarettes on the table. He stuck one behind his ear and pinched the other between his lips.

"Two, when travelling," I said.

Tuukula smiled, and then excused himself to go for a smoke on the deck. I heard the patter of Luui's small feet as she left the children's play area to join her father outside. The wind tugged at her hair and curled the smoke from Tuukula's cigarette over the railings. I felt a lump in my throat as I watched father and daughter teasing each other on the deck. There might be sixty-six years between them, but I struggled to think of another father and daughter that could be closer. I wondered about my own father, but having never met him, I struggled to recall his face. I shrugged and reached for my coffee, sipping at it as we sailed south to Maniitsoq.

I left Tuukula and Luui at the airport in Maniitsoq, peeling Luui's hands from my neck before kissing her cheek and promising that we would see each other again.

"Soon," Tuukula said.

"I hope so," I said.

My flight landed first, and I joined the other passengers as they boarded the plane, then turned to wave as Luui squeezed past the Air Greenland service staff to shout one last goodbye.

I slept on the plane, waking first as the wheels bumped down on the runway in Nuuk, and then again when the stewardess gently rubbed my shoulder.

"You're home," she said.

"Yes."

I was the last to leave the plane, leaning into the wind at door of the Dash 7, before climbing down the steps to walk to the airport building. I smiled as

I spotted the same police officer I had seen on leaving Nuuk, drawing closer as the lines of passengers arriving and departing merged in the tiny Arctic airport.

"I'm Petra," I said, pressing my hand into his. "We saw each other a few days ago."

"*Iiji*," he said.

"And your name?"

"Maratse," he said, with a brief dip of his head.

The End

Acknowledgements

As with many of my novels and novellas, I would be lost without the support and editing skills of Isabel Muir. Isabel writes cosy mysteries under her pen name *Isabella Muir*.

Special mention for help in writing *The Girl with the Raven Tongue* goes to my mother. As a trained speech and language therapist, my mum provided lots of answers to my *what if?* questions. However, the accuracy of the information about cleft lips and cleft palates, and the plausibility of a young girl training herself to speak by mimicking ravens, rests on my shoulders alone, as it was me who chose to incorporate a few facts here, while adding heaps of dramatic licence there.

As with so many of my Greenland stories, they are deeply personal in the sense that I learned so much from the Greenlandic people, and the environment of Greenland, during the seven years I lived there. *The Girl with the Raven Tongue*, however, takes on an added personal dimension, when I say that I was born with a *bifid uvula* (also known as a cleft uvula). It's the thing that hangs down in the back of your throat. Mine is split, or forked. According to my mother, I was just a hair's breadth away from having a cleft lip and cleft palate. Apart from being a constant source of amusement and interest for my mother's speech therapist friends, as a child I often experienced problems eating, with food going up my nose instead of down my throat. Swallowing tablets is still problematic. As is laughing when eating   but when isn't it?

While I can't pretend to have experienced the challenges of growing up with a cleft lip or cleft palate, it did make the story more interesting to write.

Lastly, I am very excited about the next novella in the Greenland Missing Persons series: *The Shiver in the Arctic*.

Chris
July 2020
Denmark

About the Author

Christoffer Petersen is the author's pen name. He lives in Denmark. Chris started writing stories about Greenland while teaching in Qaanaaq, the largest village in the very north of Greenland – the population peaked at 600 during the two years he lived there. Chris spent a total of seven years in Greenland, teaching in remote communities and at the Police Academy in the capital of Nuuk.

Chris continues to be inspired by the vast icy wilderness of the Arctic and his books have a common setting in the region, with a Scandinavian influence. He has also watched enough Bourne movies to no longer be surprised by the plot, but not enough to get bored.

You can find Chris in Denmark or online here:

www.christoffer-petersen.com

By the Same Author

THE GREENLAND CRIME SERIES
featuring Constable David Maratse
SEVEN GRAVES, ONE WINTER Book 1
BLOOD FLOE Book 2
WE SHALL BE MONSTERS Book 3
INSIDE THE BEAR'S CAGE Book 4
WHALE HEART Book 5

Short Stories from the same series

KATABATIC
CONTAINER
TUPILAQ
THE LAST FLIGHT
THE HEART THAT WAS A WILD GARDEN
QIVITTOQ
THE THUNDER SPIRITS
ILULIAQ
SCRIMSHAW
ASIAQ
CAMP CENTURY
INUK
DARK CHRISTMAS
POISON BERRY
NORTHERN MAIL
SIKU

VIRUSI
THE WOMEN'S KNIFE
ICE, WIND & FIRE

THE GREENLAND TRILOGY
featuring Konstabel Fenna Brongaard
THE ICE STAR Book 1
IN THE SHADOW OF THE MOUNTAIN Book 2
THE SHAMAN'S HOUSE Book 3

MADE IN DENMARK
Short Stories featuring Milla Moth set in Denmark
DANISH DESIGN Story 1

THE POLARPOL ACTION THRILLERS
featuring Sergeant Petra "Piitalaat" Jensen,
Etienne Gagnon, Hákon Sigurðsson & more
NORTHERN LIGHT Book 1
MOUNTAIN GHOST Book 2

THE DETECTIVE FREJA HANSEN SERIES
set in Denmark and Scotland
FELL RUNNER Introductory novella
BLACKOUT INGÉNUE

THE WOLF CRIMES SERIES
set in Denmark, Alaska and Ukraine
PAINT THE DEVIL Book 1
LOST IN THE WOODS Book 2
CHERNOBYL WOLVES Book 3

THE WHEELMAN SHORTS
Short Stories featuring Noah Lee set in Australia

PULP DRIVER Story 1

THE DARK ADVENT SERIES
featuring Police Commissioner
Petra "Piitalaat" Jensen set in Greenland
THE CALENDAR MAN Book 1
THE TWELFTH NIGHT Book 2
INVISIBLE TOUCH Book 3
NORTH STAR BAY Book 4

UNDERCOVER GREENLAND
featuring Eko Simigaq and Inniki Rasmussen
NARKOTIKA Book 1

CAPTAIN ERRONEOUS SMITH
featuring Captain Erroneous Smith
THE ICE CIRCUS Book 1

THE BOLIVIAN GIRL
a hard-hitting military and political thriller series
THE BOLIVIAN GIRL Book 1

GUERRILLA GREENLAND
featuring Constable David Maratse
ARCTIC STATE Novella 1
ARCTIC REBEL Novella 2

GREENLAND MISSING PERSONS novellas
featuring Constable Petra "Piitalaat" Jensen
THE BOY WITH THE NARWHAL TOOTH
THE GIRL WITH THE RAVEN TONGUE
THE SHIVER IN THE ARCTIC
THE FEVER IN THE WATER

Printed in Great Britain
by Amazon